The Wind in the Willows

THE WILD WOOD

Based on the original story by Kenneth Grahame

Retold by Andrea Stacy Leach
Illustrated by Holly Hannon

McClanahan Book Company, Inc.
New York

The Mole had long wanted to meet the Badger. But whenever the Mole mentioned his wish to the Water Rat, the Rat tried to change his mind.

"Couldn't you invite him to dinner?" asked the Mole.

"He wouldn't come," replied the Rat. "Badger hates invitations and dinner and that sort of thing."

"Well then, suppose we go and call on *him*," suggested the Mole.

"O, I'm sure he wouldn't like that," said the Rat, quite alarmed. "He's very shy. Besides, he lives in the very middle of the Wild Wood."

"You told me that the Wild Wood was all right," said the Mole.

"O, I know. So it is," replied the Rat. "But it's a long way. He'll be coming along if you'll wait quietly."

But the Badger never came along.

One winter afternoon, when Rat was dozing by the fire, Mole slipped outside.

The country lay bare and leafless around him. The air was cold and still. He walked cheerfully on toward the Wild Wood.

At first there was nothing to alarm him. Twigs crackled under his feet, logs tripped him, and shapes in the forest resembled familiar things. But it was all fun and exciting.

Then it began to grow darker. The trees

crouched nearer and nearer, and holes made ugly mouths at him. Everything was very still.

It was over his shoulder that Mole first thought he saw a face. A little wedge-shaped face, looking out at him from a hole.

He hurried on, telling himself not to imagine things. He passed another hole, and then—yes!—no!—yes! Certainly a little narrow face with hard eyes had flashed from a hole and was gone.

Suddenly, every hole seemed to possess a face. There were hundreds of them—all hard-eyed, evil, and sharp.

If only he could get away from the holes in the banks, Mole thought, there would be no more faces.

But as he left the path, the pattering began.

He thought it was only falling leaves at first. Then the sound grew and he knew it was the pat-pat-pat of little feet.

As he stood listening, a rabbit ran toward him muttering, "Get out of here!"

The noise increased until the whole wood seemed to be running, hunting, closing in. Mole ran too, although he didn't know where to go.

At last he found shelter in the deep, dark hollow of an old beech tree. He lay there panting and trembling. Now he knew the terrible thing the other animals had met here. The Rat had vainly tried to shield him from it—the Terror of the Wild Wood!

Meanwhile, the Rat, warm and comfortable, dozed by the fire. He awoke suddenly and looked around for Mole. He listened for a while. The house seemed very quiet.

"Where are you, Mole?" Rat asked. There was no answer. Rat was puzzled. He got up from his chair and went out into the hall. But the Mole was not there.

"Mole!" he called out. Then he noticed Mole's cap was missing from its peg.

The Rat went outside and examined the muddy ground. He could see that Mole's tracks ran in the direction of the Wild Wood.

Rat looked serious for a minute or two. Then he re-entered the house, strapped a belt around his waist, and shoved a pair of pistols into it. Taking a heavy club, he set off for the Wild Wood.

It was already getting dark when he reached the wood. He plunged in, looking anxiously for signs of his friend. Here and there, wicked little faces popped out of holes, but vanished at the sight of the Rat with his pistols and club.

He made his way through the wood, all the time calling out, "Moley, Moley, Moley! Where are you? It's me—it's Rat!"

At last he heard an answering cry. Guided by the sound, he made his way to the hollow of the old beech tree.

There he found the Mole, exhausted and still trembling. "O, Rat!" he cried, "I've been so frightened!"

"O, I understand," said the Rat. "But you shouldn't have gone and done it, Mole. We river-bankers hardly ever come here by ourselves," explained the Rat. "If we have to come, we come in couples, at least. Now then, we really must start for home while there is still a little light left."

"Dear Ratty," said the Mole, "I'm so sorry, but I'm exhausted. You must let me rest a little longer and get my strength back."

The Rat agreed and soon the Mole fell
asleep under the dry leaves. The Rat waited
patiently until the Mole finally awoke. Then the
Rat went to the entrance of their retreat and
stuck his head out.

"What's up, Ratty?" asked Mole.

"Snow is up," replied Rat, "or rather, down.
It's snowing hard."

"We must get started," said Rat. "I'm afraid

I don't know exactly where we are. The snow makes everything look different."

They set out bravely. They held on to each other, and pretended to be cheerful. But an hour later, they were depressed and weary.

The snow was getting so deep that they could hardly drag their little legs through it. There seemed to be no end to this wood, and no beginning. And worst of all, no way out.

Suddenly, the Mole tripped and fell forward with a squeal. "O, my leg!" he cried.

"Poor old Mole!" said the Rat kindly. "Let's have a look. Hmm, looks like you've cut your shin on something metal. Funny!"

After bandaging Mole's shin, Rat began scraping in the snow. Suddenly, he cried, "Hooray! Come and see, Moley!"

Mole hobbled up to the spot and had a good look. "Why, it's a door-scraper."

"Now look here," said the Rat, "dig and hunt around if you want to sleep dry and warm tonight." So Mole scraped busily too. After ten minutes of hard work, Rat's club struck something that sounded hollow. He stuck a paw through the snow to feel it.

The two animals continued scraping and digging till at last the results of their efforts could be seen.

In the side of what looked like a snowbank stood a little door painted dark green.

"Ratty! You're a wonder!" Mole cried. He fell backwards in surprise and delight. By the moonlight they read the brass plate next to the bellpull:

MR. BADGER

When Badger opened the door, he said, "Well, well, come in out of the cold!"

Rat and Mole were safe and warm at last.